THE

Adventures of Mar

A short story

By

Lamar Asher

Published by

Volution Arts

ISBN: 978-1-9998677-0-6

DEDICATION

For my wife, Carol.

May our journey together always be filled
with love and adventure.

CONTENTS

ACKNOWLEDGMENTS

There have been many people who have supported me through the writing of this book. There have been even more that have helped me to get to the place where I could write this book.

I would like to thank my parents who have propelled me to the place I am today.
I thank Carol, my wife. This book would not exist without her. She is always encouraging me in writing and supporting me in fulfilling the dreams I have.
I thank Daniel and Jerome, for those late night debates and 'deep and meaningful conversations'. Those were the discussions that helped bring depth and shape to the stories I write today. I would also like to thank Andre and Phinehas. They consistently dare me to dream and to achieve.

I also thank God. He is the source of my inspiration and the true author.

Lastly, I would like to thank you, the reader, for reading this short story.
I hope you enjoy it.

Chapter 1: Mar vs The Train

Chuka-Chuka... Chuka-Chuka... Chuka-Chuka. He could hear the sound of a train.

'Was it the train?' He thought.

His ears were throbbing. No! it was the sound of his heart. He suddenly became aware that his heart was pumping furiously to keep him going. His body ached and he felt the sweat dripping from his head.

Mark opened his eyes, remembering his despair. He was in a train station bent over with his hands on his knees gasping for air. He looked up only to see the platform where his train had just departed.

'I've missed it!' He thought. He couldn't believe it. Five more seconds and he would have been in a very different frame of mind to what he was in now.

'Sorry about your train,' a lady said pausing to see if he was okay. 'Is there another one?'

'No,' Mark gasped catching his breath. 'That was the last one.'

'Where were you heading?'

'Scotland… Glasgow.' He managed to say through his deep breaths. She did not reply. The expression on her face said it all. Mark was in Grand Central Station in Birmingham, almost three hundred miles away. That train had been the last of the very few that took the five-hour journey into the largest city in Scotland.

'Yep, far away...' Mark said.

'I'm sorry,' and with that, she continued down the platform.

'What am I going to do?' Mark thought. *'She will be there waiting for me.'* Worry started to overwhelm him. *'But I can't miss the train. I won't let her down.'*

The 'her' Mark was talking about was his girlfriend. It had been two years since they had been together and he had known her for a few years before that too. This weekend was their anniversary, so the train that had left was a train Mark couldn't afford to miss. Mark's worrying turned into frustration, and then into anger. Mark didn't know what had over taken him, for he now stood up.

'I won't miss this weekend!' he spurted.

His feet began moving, one in front of the other.

'Hey!' People were screaming out, scuffling out of the way alarmed, as he started to run forward.

'*They should be,*' thought Mark as he fell victim to his own body, jumping down onto the tracks and into the tunnel chasing the departing train.

'*What am I doing?*' He thought, but he didn't have time to answer the question. He had a different problem to think about now. He had run far into the tunnel and now a bright light glared back at him.

'A train!' Mark now fought against his momentum, his body began to regain sanity but it was too late. This train would reach him before he could even stop.

He raised his hands in front of his eyes as the light blinded everything.

Chapter 2: Mar vs Laedon

Mark woke up to faint sounds and a strange smell.
This was not an environment that he recognised

'Wha-, What is that?'

Mark felt something wet against his face.

He opened his eyes and jumped back as he saw what
he recognised to be a lion staring him straight in the
face.

'Whoa!' He exclaimed, scurrying backwards.

'Whoa!' The lion yelled too, springing back behind a

5

tree.

'Wait…. Did the lion just scream too?' Mark

thought. After a moment, which to Mark seemed like

hours, he realised the lion wasn't approaching him but

just watching him.

The initial shock started to wear off; Mark took a

quick glance at his surroundings.

He was in a large green field with the grass only

being a few inches high. He felt a cool summer breeze

passing over him. The sky above was clear and sunny.

Where was he?

The lion took a cautious step forward bringing

Mark's focus to the main danger at hand. This time, the

lion merely paused when Mark started. It seemed to be

getting more confident.

'It's probably realising that there would be nothing I

could do if it wanted to eat me. I'm here, alone and

helpless.' Mark thought to himself.

The lion took another step forward.

'Wait!' Mark held up his hand. Who knows why he thought he could stop the lion by frantic movements. In fact, wasn't that the one thing he was not supposed to do? Mark scurried to his feet making an awkward stance not really knowing how to defend himself.

'Wait? I won't hurt you…'

Mark still stood there, frozen awkwardly, looking at the face of the lion surrounded by a golden mane, before he came to terms with what had just happened.

'You... You can talk?!?!' Mark said.

'Sure, I can!' The lion assumed a seated position with his head tilted sideways. If lions could pull a face, Mark would have thought the lion looked confused that such a question had to be asked. 'You can talk.' The lion chuckled and started to move towards him.

'But...how can you speak?'

'How can you speak?' The lion replied now circling him as if it was inspecting him. 'You just move your mouth, throw out some air and voila! A sound we can understand.'

'But you're not supposed to.'

The lion laughed again.

'You are a strange one. "Not supposed to?"' It sniggered, trying to mimic Mark's voice. 'I've been speaking for a long time, mister. Why? Am I not supposed to?'

'This is so weird. Where am I?'

'You are in a field'

'But where is this field?'

'...here.'

'Yes! but...' Mark said in frustration trying not to raise his voice. 'This location. What is this place called?'

'Oooh. Why didn't you say so? This is the land of Lege.'

'Lege?' This conversation was not helping Mark at all.

'Yes, I can tell by your questions you aren't from around here.' The lion stopped in front of him. 'I've never seen a being like you before. But then I see new beings often. Like the other day, I saw this creature. It looked like me but he was smaller, his nose was longer and had this nasty habit of sticking his tongue out! Gross!'

'Wait so I'm in Lege? Talking to a lion,'

'Laedon.'

'What?'

'That's my name, Laedon.'

'Leedon?'

'No lay-don. My parents wanted a girl and to call her Leia but I guess they had to comprise. What is your name?'

'Me? I'm Mark.'

'Mar?'

'No Mark. Mar-Kuh. Mark!'

'Muh...Mar'

'No there's a K. Say muh'

'Muh'

'Ark'

'Ark'

'Muh-Ark. Mark!'

'Mar'

'Oh, forget it!' Mark collapsed back onto the floor staring up at the clear skies. He tried to get his head round it. This was impossible. But the last thing he remembered was. 'The train!' He yelled. 'I think I was hit by a train!'

'Ooo a train!?' Laedon jumped close. 'What's that? Is it still here? I've never seen one before. If it hit you maybe we should catch it and teach it a lesson!'

'Catch it? Oh, I missed the train. I need to get to Glasgow.'

'Glasgow? Never heard of it.'

'Why does that not surprise me.'

'But the ancient tree, he would know...'

Mark sat up suddenly. 'The ancient tree?'

'Yeah, he usually has all the answers. You know. He's been around a lot.'

'You mean he's been around a long time.'

'Yeah... and all over the lands. He would know. I know where he is now. I can take you to him. Come on!' Laedon tugged at Mark's sleeve. Mark stood up.

'This is weird. A talking Lion, a talking and

apparently walking tree?' Mark followed after the prancing lion who headed into a forest at the edge of the field.

'Come on Mar! The tree isn't going to wait around all day. He has places to be!'

Chapter 3: Mar vs The Tree

'Here he is,' Laedon announced running up to a large
Oak tree. It looked totally normal. Like any other Oak
tree apart from its wide trunk. Mark approached the tree
and started to inspect it. It had three holes probably
where birds made their home and its roots dug deep into
the soil.

'Are you sure this is the right tree?' Mark said to
Laedon.

'I'm sure of it Mar!' Laedon stood on his hind legs

and put his paws on the tree. 'Hey, Mr Tree! Ancient Tree. We need your help with something.'

Mark continued peering at the tree as Laedon continued to yell.

'Mr Ancient Tree!'

Mark took a closer look at the holes and jumped back. It moved!

The tree groaned as the branches quivered. The roots under Mark shifted and he staggered back as it seemed like the tree stretched and expanded.

'Who disturbs me!?' The tree yawned. Mark realised that the holes he had looked at were the trees eyes and mouth.

'You know who it is.' Leadon blurted as he ran to Marks side. 'I have a visitor for you.'

'Oh, it is you, little one.' The tree twisted, Mark assumed, to face them. 'My, my, it has been a while.'

'Yes, sir, 312 days and no longer counting! Anyway, my friend here needs some help he's lost and-'

'I'm sorry to rush you,' Mark interrupted. 'But I need to know how to leave this place. You see I was running down a tunnel and then I think a train hit me and I woke up here. All I want to do is reach Glasgow.' Mark stopped speaking, expecting an answer from the tree. Only, it didn't respond. It just sat there suspended. Just as he was about to give up hope the tree started talking again.

'Yes... Yes-'

'Yes! There is an exit?' Mark cried out, his heart welling up inside him with excitement.

'-Yes, young lion. It has been many days.'

Mark sighed in despair.

'You can't talk too quick with the tree Mar,' Laedon whispered to him. 'He is old and slow but he is very wise. Have some patience.' Laedon sat down not responding to the tree's comment but waited till it spoke again.

'Ooh, a friend you say,' The tree groaned more as it leaned forward. 'Ah, you are not of this world are you diligent one? Diligent I say because you are. Your path has many obstacles but you will persist still.'

Mark was about to speak but Laedon shook his head. The tree continued.

'I have travelled these lands for two millennia and have only known one other like you. You have come after him and yet, he is after you. Your paths continually cross and they always will. He knows the path you take and spoke to me these things regarding you.

'You have many adventures ahead in this land. Years may see you here. But for today, your destiny leads you to the edge of this land. Its end is what I should say.'

The tree then bellowed, almost ignoring his visitors.

'To leave this world and return to your own,

You will need Heaven's Eyes in the scaled one's

home.

But now realise that your path whether straight or

bent,

an old mysterious magic has now caught your scent.'

The tree leaned back and stiffened. There was a

moment of silence.

'Well, thanks for that Mr. Tree, we'll be on our

way!' Laedon went to walk off. 'Let's go Mar!'

'Wait!' Mark shouted. 'Some sort of magic is

following us? And I'll be here for years?! I can't. I can't

stay here for years I need to be in Glasgow this

weekend!' The tree didn't respond. It was now still

again just like any other tree.

'Mar,' Laedon called out to him. Mark didn't want to

listen. He wanted answers and all he got was more questions and now the tree just stood there.

Mark decided to wait for a reply. Maybe it was still trying to process the questions he barraged it with. He waited a little longer but the tree didn't move. It was obviously finished with him.

'Mar,' Laedon called out to him again. 'You're not going to get anything more out of him. Once he's done, he's done.'

'But I have more questions! He didn't really answer anything.'

Leadon ran behind Mark and pushed him forward with his head. 'Come on Mar!'

Mark relented and started moving. Was he any closer to getting out of this strange land? He turned back to look at the old oak tree. Only it wasn't there. The ground didn't even have any evidence that the tree had been there.

'Where did it go?' Mark paused.

'I told you he likes to travel,' Laedon said, obviously being entertained by Mark's reaction to things that were clearly normal for him.

'Strange...'

'Alright mister, let's get going. Onwards to Lege's End!'

Chapter 4: Mar vs The Troll

Mark stood at the edge of a river bank. Beyond him laid another foreign land that probably held more obstacles before he could leave this world. This bank was the end of Lege. He had been travelling over a day now. *'Saturday. It's Saturday,'* He thought. *'Will I ever make it out of here?'* The land was still strange and just when he thought he was getting familiar, something else would come and surprise him. It was a good thing he had Leadon who had never left his side.

Leadon was a peculiar character. Even in the dangers that presented themselves to them, the lion was strangely relaxed and optimistic. Mark doubted he would ever see him frown. The lion just took each moment at a time and seemed to enjoy every bit of it. If it wasn't for Leadon who knows what state Mark would have been in now. Maybe still in the centre of the field lost in despair? No, he would have tried to get out. But, it might have taken him longer to get any sort of bearing or information.

The ancient tree's information was fragmented and it had frustrated Mark for hours but as Leadon pointed out, he now knew that he could get back to his world and also had a direction.

'The scaled one,' Mark thought back to the words the tree had said. *'Is that some sort of serpent?'* Leadon did not know either. Out of all the wild things he saw he had not seen a snake of any kind. It was most likely that

whatever creature it was, it lay beyond Lege. This land that was in front of them now.

'So, this is it?' Mark said. 'Lege's End.'

'I have never travelled out this far before.' Laedon walked to the edge of the river and dipped his nose in before lapping up some with his tongue. 'This is exciting!'

Mark caught sight of a bridge off to the right. 'This will take us to the other side.' He called out to Laedon and they both approached the bridge.

The bridge was very broad and made of a strong wood. 'I wonder who built it,' Mark thought.

Mark took his first step onto the bridge while Laedon ran ahead in excitement. Laedon's youthful spirit made him smile. As he ran his fingers along the edge of the bridge he noticed strange engravings along it. 'Was it letters, patterns, or both?' Mark looked closer and followed the lines and swirls.

Suddenly he heard a loud splash then a thud. Laedon yelped and ran back towards him. Mark's attention was brought to the floor of the bridge which now seemed to shift under him trying to throw him off balance. As he got his footing, his eyes trailed back up the bridge to find large feet; then a large belly; followed by a large head. It looked like a troll. At least fifteen feet in height. It was a wonder that the bridge did not collapse under his weight. But the thing that worried Mark the most was that the troll had a massive club in its hand which rested on his shoulder.

Laedon was now behind Mark but he still hadn't lost his smile. *'Was he enjoying this?'* Mark thought because he wasn't. He was trying to keep his legs from buckling under him. This thing. It was huge and it looked angry.

'Turn back!' It boomed. 'You cannot pass this

bridge.' Mark went to take a step back but Laedon nudged him forward.

'Umm, hi,' Mark said clearing his through. 'I err … We need to get to the other side. See, I'm not from around here…'

'Did you not hear me?' The troll bellowed. 'I am the troll of this bridge and you will not pass. Turn back!'

Mark grew frustrated. *'How are we going to get past this troll? Could we out run him? Sneak past him? What are we going to do?'*

'Excuse me, sir,' Laedon now stepped forward. 'I can't help but notice that you seem a bit upset.'

'Laedon!' Mark objected but the lion didn't listen. The troll now glared at the little lion.

'What is your name?' Laedon said calmly.

'Did Laedon think he could talk to this thing?' Mark was terrified, his heart in his throat. Beads of sweat

started to form on his forehead as the lion and the troll seemed to be in a standoff.

'John,' the troll said. 'My name is John.'

What followed, Mark would never believe. If anything could make his experience throughout this land any stranger, it would be witnessing a talking lion giving therapy to a gigantic troll.

'This is ridiculous' Mark thought. But he had been so surprised by the whole scene that he hadn't noticed that the two were now staring at him.

'Oh, hi.' He said nervously. 'Did you say something?' The troll had been sitting during the talk with Laedon and had rested the club on his lap; it didn't make Mark feel any easier. He didn't think anything would at this point.

'I just told John here about our situation and he said he is willing to strike a deal with us for helping him out with his problem.' Mark resisted his curiosity about the conversation he had missed, on remembering that the two were waiting for a response.

'Oh right. Yes, I would appreciate that.'

'I'll tell you what,' the troll got up onto his feet. 'I'll let you pass if you can solve this riddle. That way if anyone asks, I didn't just let you go past.'

'That sounds great,' Laedon blurted before Mark could ask 'What if we get it wrong?' But he was sure that was a question he would rather not know the answer to.

'Okay, here it is.' The troll flung his club onto his shoulder and took in a long deep breath then released it as if to ponder on how best to say the next few words.

'A three-worded phrase is what I need,

See it as a price or a cost, that which kills jealousy and greed.

When taken it's a chain, when given in love it's a gift indeed,

But only in one's hand does it truly mean you are freed.'

The troll smiled. 'What is your answer?'

Mark and Laedon had been thinking about the answer. They had narrowed it down to be a quantity of something, but it could not be money or even material as they fuel greed. They ruled out the answer being love. That could be quantized but even then, you cannot give love in love. And only in one's hand…

Mark got it.

'Err John, I know your answer!'

'Yes, what is it?'

'All of me!'

Mark didn't know what to make of the troll's face. What expressions did trolls make anyway when they wanted to display an emotion? Mark stood still waiting for the troll's response.

'Well, I say,' John said. 'Marvellous! You are right! You can pass.' Laedon celebrated. John stepped aside and summoned them to walk past. 'I know what it is you seek by the way.' John said as Mark reached the other side. 'Follow the path in the woods and turn neither left nor right. It will take you to the base of a mountain. There is a cave there where the scaled one lives. I don't know what it is but be careful. I have not seen anyone enter and come back out.'

'Thanks!' Laedon shouted back. 'Take care, John!'

With that Mark and Laedon began their journey again crossing over into a new land.

'You know we didn't find out the name of this land.' Mark said.

'And you need to tell me how you got that answer.' Laedon replied.

Amidst their conversation, the two didn't even realise that there was something close lurking behind them as they entered the woods. The mysterious magic was close on their trail.

Chapter 5: Mar vs The Magic

'Here is the cave, Mar!' Laedon said running up to the entrance.

'Wait, Laedon,' Mark yelled out. The last thing he wanted was the 'scaled one' knowing that they were there. 'We don't even have a plan!'

'Yeah, we do. We just have to grab Heaven's Eyes and then we skedaddle.'

'Sshh!' Mark put his fingers to the lion's lips and realised that it might not be the best idea. In his world that would just be teasing him with fresh food. He pulled

back his finger at the thought. 'We don't want to alert

it!' At Marks remark, Laedon composed himself. 'Now

we don't know what Heaven's Eyes are or what it looks

like.' Mark could see the thoughts register in Laedon's

mind. 'We don't even know if the scaled one is friendly

although I highly doubt that. You heard the troll. He

doesn't know of anyone who went in and has made it

out alive. We can't just rush in there.'

Mark pushed his back to the cave opening, slowly

peeking in. The entrance was a narrow tunnel. It was

dark and he couldn't see past where it started to turn.

'Alright.' Mark whispered. 'It looks like we have no

choice but to go in. But we must be extremely cautious.

That means for you to be extremely quiet Laedon.' Mark

did not know what would happen when they walked in

or what to expect. 'Let's go Laedon... Laedon!'

Mark turned around. Laedon was nowhere to be found.

'Laedon!' Mark called out.

'Mar!' A worried cry came out from the side of the mountain. He could tell that Laedon was in trouble. He darted in that direction.

When he reached he saw Laedon with his back against the wall, looking up at what seemed to be a dense cloud of dust. The dust was made up of many colours, too many for Mark to count. Flashes of lightning seemed to be erupting within it and parts of the dust formed a stream that would flow in and out of it. It was both majestic and terrifying. It was like staring into a nebula with a time-lapse.

'This can't be the scaled one,' Mark thought. *'It must be...'*

'The magic!' Laedon screamed.

Mark sprang forward and put himself between Laedon and the magic.

'Hey, stop right there and come no further!' Mark shouted, stretching out his arms. He did not know where he got the sudden courage from, but he wouldn't idly sit there and allow Laedon to be killed.

The flashes in the cloud grew more frequent. But it didn't come close. It just hung there.

'What was it doing?' Mark wondered. He could now hear the faint thunder of the flashes and the movement of the dust.

'I think you have misinterpreted the situation, Mark,' said the cloud. Its voice was deep yet soft. It was like pure notes, purer than any instrument or voice could make. 'I am not here to hurt you.'

Mark took a quick glance at Laedon, before turning back to the cloud. He would tell Laedon to run for it when the opportunity arose.

'How do I know you're telling the truth?'

'Have I not been on your tail Mark, have I not been with you all this time?' Mark didn't understand.

'I think he's telling the truth Mar.' Laedon said moving in front of Mark.

'Laedon, No!'

'Mr. Magic,' Laedon slowly approached the cloud.

'Not again,' Mark thought, *'He can't keep approaching everyone like that and expect it to solve everything...'*

The cloud rumbled, more flashing came from it. It was laughing!

'I have been called many things, but magic? That old tree can be so stubborn. Now you don't have much time. The sun will soon set and dusk will be upon you. I have revealed myself now so that you may obtain what you seek. Mark, I will tell you what you need to know.'

Mark let himself relax a little. Could he really trust this thing? He knew that going into the cave with the information he currently had was a long shot. It was likely that he wasn't going to survive.

'Okay,' he said. 'I'll listen.'

The cloud drifted away slowly and settled three metres from Mark.

'For you to return home Mark, you need Heaven's Eyes that much you know already.' Mark nodded in agreement. 'Heaven's Eyes are stones. Two in total. You will need to find them amongst the other treasures in the cave. The scaled one, that is the dragon, does not like to entertain guests so I advise you to be careful, but you can do it.'

'A dragon!?' Mark's heart sunk. It was worse than he anticipated. He would have taken a snake over a dragon.

'That is all I will reveal for now but you will find me here when you have completed this task. You will do well Mark. Trust me.'

'Wait, you're not coming with me?' Mark said, his voice wavering.

'I am.' Reassured the cloud.

'But you said you will be waiting out here?' Mark remarked.

'If I was to explain to you my definition of here you would have to relearn the definition of yours. I will be with you, Mark.'

Mark knew that was all he was going to get from him, he let out a sigh.

'Okay. Let's get those stones then.' He reluctantly stood. The sun was setting now. It would be better to go into the cave while the sun was still up. Who knows what might happen in these woods in the dark.

Laedon rose too and followed Mark, both didn't speak. What could be said of the experience they just had?

That was the magic. Well, that's what the tree had called him. He checked his hands, they were still shaking. As they reached the entrance, they both stood at opposite sides.

'Are you ready?' Mark said.

'Ready.' Laedon said.

They entered the cave.

Chapter 6: Mar vs The Dragon

'This place stinks!'

'Sshh'

'How far do you think we have to go Mar?'

'I'm not sure. Keep your voice down.'

Laedon was right, the cave smelled terrible. It wreaked of sulphur and burnt rock. As they got deeper into the mountain the temperature was also rising; Mark began to sweat.

After a few minutes into the journey, the tunnel

began to spiral and descend. It might have been a shorter walk if they weren't treating every step like it would alert the dragon to their presence. It wasn't worth the risk, they will go slow.

Suddenly the tunnel opened into a large cavern and was surrounded by light. As his eyes adjusted, Mark realised that the light was coming from the gold in the cave.

'Whoa,' Laedon said quietly. Mark signalled to him to keep quiet. Without knowledge of where the dragon was, they needed to be careful.

The source of the light came from various parts of the cave where lava had broken the floor's surface and created miniature pools.

The sight of the cavern was magnificent. Never had Mark seen so much gold. But that was not what he was here for. He crept further in, finding a pillar.

'This should hide me from where the dragon is.' He thought.

He held up his hand to tell Laedon to wait at the entrance.

'Now to find the dragon.' Mark peered around one side of the pillar. He could make out that the cavern was large and dipped further, deeper than anyone could venture. *'Please don't let the stones be deep inside this cave.'*

CLANG!!

Mark jumped, his heart racing, as he saw at the entrance a large amount of gold shifting, causing an avalanche. The noise echoed down the tunnel. He looked up to see Laedon further in by a series of golden statues looking apologetic.

'Laedon!' Mark said silently with his eyes. They both held their breath as the noise subsided leaving a

tangible silence.

Mark exhaled. This means the dragon could be deep in...

More clanging. Mark's hairs stood up on end, as deep in the tunnel he could see gold rising then falling. Lights trickled up and down the walls as the gold rolled off the black scaled back of the beast. Its head turned slowly but confidently. The eyes opened in Mark and Laedon's direction. As it fully emerged its stomach started to glow. It's breath deepening as it started its walk towards them. It knew exactly where they were. Mark knew what was coming next. The pillar should give him cover but Laedon...

'Laedon!' Mark shouted. 'Go back up now! Run!' For once thankfully, Laedon didn't hesitate and darted back up the tunnel.

The flames came.

Mark pulled himself in as he felt the fire come towards him. He tightly shut his eyes feeling the heat surge past the pillar like a river. Even though his eyes were shut, all Mark could see was white light.

As it faded, Mark opened his eyes and found the dragon right next to him. But it didn't pay him any mind. Then he realised. It was going for Leadon, who was still running up the tunnel. Mark hopped out of cover.

'Hey! Hey, you! I'm here. I'm here!'

But it didn't look at him. It was going to send flames up the tunnel and he couldn't stop it.

And so the dragon did. It breathed out its flames. Mark could only hope that Laedon made it in time. Mark quickly glanced back into the tunnel and now noticed a white sparkle.

'That could be the Heaven's Eyes!' He thought.

There were only a few pillars between them and his position. He could make it.

He ran for the next pillar and ducked for cover before the dragon turned to give his focus back to the intruder in the room.

'No one sees and survives.' It spoke. This did not surprise Mark. But the sinister sound of it sent a chill down his spine. 'Bound they come, bound they go. It's never the fire that does the blow.'

Mark still crouched behind the pillar but he knew he couldn't stay there. It would find him and get him. Another light caught his eye. It was from the dragon. On the left ankle was a golden chain. It was bound!

But that didn't matter. It gave him no advantage, neither did staying in cover. His chances were the same whether or not the dragon knew where he was. Staying in the same place, however, was suicide.

Mark ran to the next pillar, making it just in time before more flames raged past it.

'Many come down. And all never leave.

They're trapped here by their guilt or greed.'

Mark heard it coming towards him.

'I'm not like the others!' Mark said as he ran to the next cover.

'Oh? Vanity is a form of greed.

Your fate in here is sealed indeed'

'I'm not here for your gold!' Mark shouted back.

'Then what fuels your goal if not pride or treasure.

What are you risking your life for? Can it measure?'

Mark was close now. The stones were in sight.

'Love. Love is why I am here. I have not paused to settle in this land. This is not my home. I have to get back to the one I love.'

'Love? Love!? A foolish notion and thought.

One cooked up to bind, control and thwart!'

Mark waited for the next flames to pass and made a dive for the stones. He held them in his hands and rose to his feet. Looking up he saw the Dragon standing over him. Its belly glowing, smoke rising from its nostrils.

Mark stood tall, finding an unnatural confidence and holding the glowing stones, his mind filled with words and he shouted them out.

'The price to pay for love is grand,

a cost so high not all can stand.

A finite quantity, an infinite value.

One is required, from one it is due.

All of me, love costs. All of me it needs.

My life is the sacrifice, love needs to succeed.

It's my gift to her, and from Christ, it comes from.

All of me in him, that love will overcome!'

'A fine statement made,' said the dragon. 'But I think you are a liar!

The truth shall be revealed through flames and fire!'

The dragon breathed its fire right at Mark.

Chapter 7: Mar vs The End

Mark opened his eyes and realised the fire wasn't harming him. In fact, it was parting around him. The dragon looked astonished. He breathed out fire again but still, it didn't affect Mark.

Mark, confused, looked at the stones in his hands. It must be the Heaven's Eyes. He decided not to waste any time and ran towards the exit, the dragon still on his tail. The dragon was screaming at him, breathing fire but Mark dodged, leapt and dived over the treasures in the cave.

As Mark headed through the exit, the dragon let out a mighty roar and jetted out a sea of flames through the tunnel. Mark continued running not slowing down as the flames seemed to surround him in the tunnel.

He toppled out the exit lying face up at the red sky. Smoke and dust bellowing out the tunnel. As he caught his breath he smiled at the familiar voice that greeted him.

'Mar! You made it. I was so worried. What happened?' Mark tried to speak but he was too out of breath, leaving the question unanswered.

'I knew you could do it, Mark.' Mark sat up hearing the familiar pure toned voice of the magic.

'Thank you,' Mark finally let out. He opened his hands to show the two stones. 'These stones protected me from the flames.' He rose to his feet. 'So... So these will take me home?' He looked up at the magic which now drew close to him. Laedon was by his side.

'Yes, they will, but we don't have much time, it is nearly dusk. Come here so we may begin.' Mark approached the cloud. As the Sun went down the magic seemed more vibrant now. It was a wonder how they never knew it was following them.

'Before we start...' Mark faced Laedon. 'Thank you. You have been such a great companion. I wouldn't have wanted to walk this journey with anyone else.'

'You're not so bad yourself Mar.' Laedon replied.

'What will happen to Laedon? How will he get back?' Mark asked the magic.

'I will take him. Are you ready?'

Mark nodded.

'Then hold up the stones to me.'

Mark obeyed and as he did they started to glow

brighter and then they began to vibrate. Mark looked up. The world started to shake violently and seemed to get darker. He felt as if the world was moving from under his feet. It was literally slipping away.

'Bye Mar!' Laedon shouted.

'Bye,' Mark said but he now felt a million miles away from his brief companion. 'Bye...'

Mark opened his eyes feeling vibrations against his head. He was leaning on a window. As he became more aware of his surroundings, he realised he was sitting in a seat. Out the of window, he saw lots of green fields passing by.

He was on a train.

Mark strained trying to remember what happened. *'That was a strange dream,'* He thought. *'But I vividly remember missing the train. Was that all part of the dream?'*

He had boarded the train, only just and must have fallen asleep at the beginning of the journey.

'Next stop Glasgow! All change please! All change!' The announcement came out the speaker.

'So, it was all a dream?' He thought. But it had felt so real. As the train came to a halt at Glasgow station, Mark grabbed his bag and got ready to leave the train...

Epilogue

Dear beloved,

It was a wild journey I had before I saw you.

I dreamt of a lion who I later realised was my

childish self and he guided me through various trials.

I witnessed and experienced very strange things in

that world. I encountered a tree with a vast amount of

knowledge, but it only gave me answers in part. It's

funny how it's the first thing we draw on, knowledge.

But it only leaves us with more questions than answers.

Science finds it hard to explain what love is because love is on a higher plane. An eternal thing rather than temporal. Can love really be explained so easily? Knowledge can only take us so far.

I encountered a troll that threatened my journey and the success of my quest. Posing questions that could not be answered right away. The only way I could succeed was to change my attitude and engage with the task at hand. Like when you get to a bridge and you realise that to cross, it will take all of you; nothing less. We find this in our relationship. The point where we decide that we are all in. For us, I crossed that bridge a long time ago.

But with all this experience, knowledge and commitment it was still not enough. 'magic' is a funny term. It is often used in fantasy to explain supernatural events that science can't explain. When I looked into the cloud that had been following me on my journey, I realised what it was. Our actual companion. The spirit of God who never leaves us or forsakes us. You see, He too brings things into view in part, only there was a key difference. He brought confidence. He gave me the relevant information and comfort. He is the one that goes before us and He is always pursuing us, seeking us to be in a relationship with God.

And finally, I realised that there are times when we are trapped in a dungeon. Whether by pride, greed or fear and it can hold us down and trap us. If we are not careful these things will lead us to our doom. But our perspective is vital in these moments; we need to look with Heaven's eyes. How does God see us? How do we see the world when we have our perspective right? Looking at things with an eternal perspective, material goods are put in their rightful place and become less important. This same perspective helps us realise that we are eternal spiritual beings, and so relationships and love become of higher importance. And fear remains as F.E.A.R: False Evidence Appearing Real.

Love has an eternal value and it is with that love that we love one another and overcome any obstacle that comes our way.

Love Mar

ABOUT THE AUTHOR

Lamar Asher was born in Birmingham, UK. He enjoys playing the piano, programming, gaming and of course, writing. Obsessed with stories since a very young age, he started creating his own in secondary school whenever he got the chance. If you were to search his house, it is likely that you could find every single 'rough book' he acquired from those days, where he stored all his story ideas.

www.ingramcontent.com/pod-product-compliance
Lightning Source LLC
Chambersburg PA
CBHW070648130626
46555CB00006B/2770